Bella's Dragon

Flyaway Frankie

Also by Chris Powling

The Conker as Hard as a Diamond

Chris Powling

Bella's Dragon

and

Flyaway Frankie

Illustrated by
Robert Bartelt

Happy Cat Books

HAPPY CAT BOOKS

Published by Happy Cat Books Ltd.
Bradfield, Essex CO11 2UT, UK

This edition published 2003
1 3 5 7 9 10 8 6 4 2

A CIP catalogue record for this book is available from the British Library

ISBN 1 903285 46 1

Printed in England

CONTENTS

BELLA'S DRAGON

For Lottie and her mum

On the coldest day of the year, a
dragon suddenly flopped into
Bella's back garden. His tail
wrapped itself round the tool
shed and his wings cast a great
shadow over the snow.

'Hello, dragon,' said Bella in
surprise.

'Hello, little girl,' said the

dragon. 'Why aren't you at school?'

'Because the boiler's broken down,' said Bella. 'It's so old, you see. All the pipes are frozen up. The teachers had to send us home.'

'Lucky you!' the dragon said.

'We're not,' said Bella. 'We like school. It's boring being at home.'

The dragon gave her a wink. 'Lucky me, then,' he said, 'because I can do with a bit of help if you're not too busy.'

'Fine,' said Bella. 'What sort of help?'

'I'm looking for a new den,' said the dragon.

'A new den?' said Bella.

'That's right,' said the dragon. 'I'm fed up with living in a cave or on top of a mountain or in some faraway place where I never get to meet anybody. It's so lonely. What I want is a dry, cosy den right here in the middle of town. Can you find one for me?'

'How much money have you got?' Bella asked.

'Money?' said the dragon. 'You mean I've got to pay?'

'Of course,' said Bella.

'But I never had to pay for my caves or my mountain-tops,' said the dragon.

'Towns are different,' Bella said.

'I see,' said the dragon huffily. 'Well, I haven't got any money, so that's that. We'll have to find somewhere that's free.'

Bella sighed and shook her head. 'We can try,' she said. 'I wish I could ask my teacher what to do, dragon. I don't think this is going to be easy.'

It wasn't easy. For a start, people stared at Bella and the dragon from the moment they saw them in the street. Of course, people didn't believe the dragon was real.

'It's a big, electric toy,' they told each other. 'Or one of those computer-robot things.'

But they still whispered and pointed fingers.

'Take no notice,' Bella said. 'They'll soon get used to you.'

'Me?' said the dragon. 'I thought they were pointing at you.'

After this, he waved a claw at them or flashed them a big, fangy grin. This soon stopped the whispering.

Bella's first stop was the estate agent.

'What's an estate agent?' the dragon wanted to know.

'He's a sort of shopkeeper who

15

sells places to live,' Bella
explained. 'You know – houses
and flats and maisonettes.'

'And dens?' asked the dragon.

'Maybe,' said Bella.

She wasn't too sure about
dens.

The estate agent wasn't too sure
about dragons, either.

'What is it?' he asked nervously.

'A big, electric toy? Or one of
those computer-robot things?'

'I'm a dragon,' said the
dragon, his huge knobbly head
poking through the doorway.
'And this is –'

'Bella,' said Bella.

'Well, you keep it under
control, whatever it is,' said the

estate agent. 'Now, how can I help?'

'I need a den for this dragon, sir,' said Bella. 'It's got to be dry and cosy and right here in the middle of town so he won't get lonely. Oh, and there's one thing

more. The den mustn't cost any money.'

'No money?'

Now it was the estate agent's turn to be huffy. 'Kindly go away, little girl,' he snapped. 'I haven't got time for jokes.'

'There's no need to be rude,' said the dragon.

And with a flick of his tongue he tipped the estate agent head first into his own wastepaper basket. They left him upside down with his legs waving in the air.

'That was naughty, dragon,' Bella scolded.

'Serve him right,' said the dragon. 'Where do we look now?'

'My teacher would tell us,' Bella said. 'Miss Baker's lovely. And she's so clever. If only school were open . . .'

'How about over there?' asked the dragon suddenly.

'There?' Bella blinked.

The dragon nodded. 'It's not perfect, Bella. I can see that. For a start, it hasn't got any walls.

But the flat roof is quite smart, isn't it? And those drink machines will be very useful when I get thirsty.'

'Those aren't drink machines,' yelped Bella. 'Those are petrol pumps!'

The dragon didn't hear her. Already he was lumbering across the road towards the garage.

Very politely, he took his place in the queue. In front of him were a girl on a motorbike and a man in a white Mini. As soon as they noticed the dragon, they decided they didn't need petrol after all.

BROOM-BROOM-BROOM they

23

went. The dragon watched them go.

'Cheerio!' called the dragon. 'What a lot of rushing about there is in a town! Now . . . shall I have a two-star drink or a four-star drink?'

He decided to have both.

Guzzle – guzzle – guzzle. Glug – glug – glug.

Bella saw the numbers whizzing round in the little windows on the petrol pumps.

'You're drinking them dry!' she exclaimed.

'Hey!' called the garage-lady. 'What kind of lorry is that? Is it a juggernaut?'

'It's a dragon,' Bella said.

'A dragon?' said the garage-
lady. 'I never heard of a lorry
with that name. Good gracious, it
hasn't even got wheels! Kindly
get it off my forecourt this
minute. Can't you see it's

frightening away all my other customers? They think it's a REAL dragon.'

'It is a real dragon,' said Bella.

'What?' said the garage-lady. 'Now don't be silly, dear . . .'

Her voice died away. This was because the dragon was so full up he gave a small dragon-size burp. A sheet of flame hissed out of his mouth. Instantly every bit of snow around the garage was turned into steam as if a cloud had crash-landed on top of them.

'I can't see a thing!' the garage-lady cried.

'We'd better get going, Bella,'

said the dragon. 'I don't think she likes you very much.'

'Me?' said Bella. 'You were causing all the trouble.'

'Trouble? What trouble?' said the dragon.

There was no chance to explain. By the time they were clear of the mist, the dragon had already spotted his next new den.

'Look,' he said. 'It's wonderful! I love it!'

'That place?' Bella gasped. 'You can't go in there!'

'Why not?' asked the dragon.

'Because it's an indoor swimming pool!' said Bella.

She knew she was wasting her

breath. All she could do was
hurry after the dragon as he
lolloped into the changing
rooms.

'Eek!' screamed the girls on one side.

'Aargh!' yelled the boys on the other side.

'Come back!' roared the attendant.

The dragon was too excited to hear him.

The swimmers were pretty excited, too, when they saw the dragon. 'It's one of those computer-robot things,' they told each other. 'Or maybe a big, electric toy.'

'But why is it here?'

'Who owns it?'

'What's it going to do?'

'Looks like it wants a swim . . .'

'A swim?'

The dragon stood on tiptoe at
the deep-end of the pool, holding
his claws straight out in front of
him. He was taller than the
diving boards. 'Want to see a
belly-flop?' he said.

'Don't do it!' Bella shouted.

Too late.

KERPLONK!

At once there wasn't a drop of
water left in the swimming pool.
Instead, it was all running down
the walls or dripping from the
ceiling. The people eating crisps
in the cafeteria were just as wet
as the people in the pool, who
were clambering out of it as fast
as they could.

'Where's everybody going?'

asked the dragon. 'Why have
you frightened them away,
Bella? This place is no good for
a den now. It's so empty and
echo-y. I'm off.'

'Wait!' Bella called out. 'That's
the way to –'

'Get a move on, Bella!'
interrupted the dragon.

And away he galloped, half
hopping, half flying.

'I can't keep up,' panted Bella.
'What would Miss Baker do, I
wonder? I know – she'd follow
his tracks in the snow.'

The tracks led straight to the
Superstore.

Was the Superstore so
crowded because it was the

coldest day of the year, do you think? There were people everywhere. The dragon couldn't possibly feel lonely here.

'Hello,' he said to the shoppers on the escalator as he went up

and they went down. 'I like a den
with a moving staircase!'

'Hello,' he said to the shoppers
in the Food Hall as he gobbled
up everything in the deep freeze.
'I like a den with a well stocked
fridge!'

'Hello,' he said to the shoppers at the checkout till as he pushed through thirty-six trollies at once. 'I like a den with my very own puffer train. Whoo-whoo!'

The Superstore customers couldn't believe their eyes. 'It's one of those big, electric toys, isn't it?' they asked each other.

'Or a computer-robot thing?'
  'No it's not,' Bella told them.
'It's a dragon, actually.'

'A dragon?' they echoed.

'A real-life dragon, yes,' said Bella. 'He wants a den here in the middle of town. I'm helping him find one.'

'A den? For a dragon? A real-life dragon?'

'That's right,' said Bella.

Everyone stared at the dragon, warily. He was hovering over the coffee shop now, with his wings spread out like a giant umbrella. His face wore a happy grin.

'This is a great den,' he said. 'If I'm careful, I can even get in a bit of flying practice. Hey, why is everybody shuffling towards the exit?'

41

'Goodbye, dragon!' they waved. 'We know you're not really real. It's some kind of joke, we reckon. But just in case . . .'

Poor dragon!

Soon the Superstore was as empty as the garage and the swimming pool. 'You've done it again, Bella,' he groaned. 'Another den ruined. I can't work out why people find you so scary.'

Bella didn't have the heart to tell him. Besides, they still had a den to find.

'This is awful,' she said, sadly. 'We're not getting anywhere. I wish I were back in school.'

'Hello, Bella,' came a voice.

Bella swung round. 'Miss Baker!' she exclaimed. 'What are you doing here?'

'I was bringing back all the stuff I bought for the end-of-term party,' said Miss Baker. 'With the school closed, we won't be needing it. Or will we? This friend of yours has just given me an idea. Are you a proper dragon, I wonder?'

'Certainly,' said the dragon.

'And what sort of den are you looking for?' asked Miss Baker.

'Somewhere dry,' said the dragon gloomily. 'And cosy. With plenty of people about so I don't get lonely. There's nowhere like that round here.'

'There is,' smiled Miss Baker. 'I know just the place.'

'You do?' said the dragon.

'It's over the road,' said Miss Baker. 'Right here in the middle of town. Come with me, please!'

Can you guess where she took them?

Of course, there were still a few problems. For instance, the caretaker had to take away the doors to the boiler-room and shift

47

out the old boiler. Also, the
dragon had to get used to
breathing very gently down the
pipes. 'I don't want to make the
school TOO hot,' he said. 'And in
Summer, I'll blow cold air
through them to cool everyone
down. What a terrific den, Miss
Baker! I'm really grateful.'

'So am I,' laughed Miss Baker.
'This is the only school in the
world that's run by dragon-
power!'

Bella laughed, too. So did all
the other kids when they came
back for the end-of-term party.
And they went on laughing every
break-time after that, because
when they went into the

playground they always had a big, electric toy to play with, or one of those computer-robot things.

Well, that's what some people thought it was.

FLYAWAY FRANKIE

For Mike and Christina

Last Tuesday, on his way to
school, Frankie met a witch. He
knew at once it would lead to
trouble.

'Hello, witch,' he said nervously.

'Hello, Frankie,' said the witch.

'How do you know what my
name is?' Frankie asked.

'How do you know I'm a witch?'

'I guessed,' said Frankie.

But he wasn't really guessing. He could tell she was a witch from her pointed hat, her black cloak and her cackly voice. Also she was holding a broom made of twigs. With clues like that wouldn't you have spotted what she was?

'You're a clever boy,' said the witch. 'Plenty of people think this is a costume for a fancy dress party.'

'Not me,' said Frankie.

'Of course not,' said the witch. 'That's because you're *special*, Frankie. You're a one-in-a-million kid, I bet!'

'Am I?'

'Certainly you are. For example,

have you noticed I'm lying
upside down in this ditch not
able to move a muscle?'

Frankie nodded. 'I was
wondering about that,' he
said.

'Smart lad,' said the witch. 'I
knew I could count on you. I've
just fallen out of the sky, you see,
and I need a bit of help. Would
you mind passing me that small
stick you're almost standing on? I
can't quite reach it from here.'

Frankie looked down. Sure
enough, there was the stick right
by his feet. 'Is it your magic
wand?' he asked.

'You could call it that,' said the
witch.

'I thought so,' said Frankie.

Frankie picked the wand up. It was like a long, bony finger. 'My teacher told us a witch is helpless without her wand,' he said. 'She reckons if you ever find a witch's wand you should always snap it in half because that takes her magic away.'

'Really?' said the witch. 'How very interesting. I'd like to meet that teacher of yours.'

'Oh, don't worry,' said Frankie, 'I don't always do what my teacher says. Here you are.'

And he flipped the wand into the witch's upside-down lap.

It was the wrong thing to do, of course. You should never, ever let a witch have her wand back. Frankie was about to find out why.

'Thank you, Frankie,' said the witch. 'What a kind lad you are. Let me show you how grateful I am. When I've waved this wand you'll be able to do something that's really, really hard, even for a witch!'

'What's that?' said Frankie in alarm.

'You'll be able to stay up in the air as long as you like,' cackled the witch. 'Maybe even longer.'

'Wait!' said Frankie.

He was too late. Already the

witch had twiddled her wand,
hopped on her broomstick and
whooshed away. All she left
behind was the echo of witchy
laughter.

Poor Frankie!

Now he was sure there was trouble coming.

At first, though, nothing much seemed to have changed – except that his journey to school didn't take as long as usual.

'It's like I'm walking on air,' said Frankie.

This was because he really was walking on air. But he didn't find this out till he was in the school playground.

'You've got taller, Frankie,' said the other kids.

'Have I?' said Frankie.

'Much taller – no, wait a minute. It's your feet, Frankie. They're not on the ground.'

'Aren't they?' said Frankie.

'You're floating, Frankie!'

Frankie saw at once they were right. There was a gap between the bottom of his shoes and the top of the playground – a gap about as high as a doorstep. Would the gap get any bigger, though?

'Quick,' said Frankie. 'Grab hold of me. I might blow away like a piece of fluff.'

'Don't worry, Frankie,' said the other kids. 'We'll look after you.'

They did, too. They took turns to stand next to him, holding him down by his arms.

'You've got a lot of friends, today, Frankie,' said the teacher who came to blow the whistle at in-time.

'Yes, Miss,' said Frankie.

And his friends went on holding him all the way to the classroom, all through the register and all through news-time. They were still holding him when they went to the Hall for assembly.

'Good morning, children,' said Mrs Jones, the headmistress.

'Good morning, Mrs Jones,' said the children. 'Good morning, teachers. Good morning, everyone.'

'We'll start with a prayer,' said Mrs Jones. 'Close your eyes,

please, and put your hands
together. You too, Frankie. And
the children each side of you.'

'But, Miss –'

'Do as you're told, Frankie. Put
your hands together, please.'

'Miss –'

'Frankie!'

Frankie did as he was told. So
did the friend on his right and so
did the friend on his left.

'Frankie,' said Mrs Jones in her
sharpest voice. 'Get your bottom
back on the floor this instant.'

'I'll try,' said Frankie.

But he couldn't. There he was,
sitting cross-legged in mid-air,
about as high as the top of a
doorway. 'Frankie, come down at

once,' Mrs Jones gasped. 'What you're doing isn't a bit clever, you know.'

It was, though. Some of the little kids even started to clap – especially when Frankie tried to dive downwards and turned a complete head-over-heels in the air. By now he was as high as the wallbars. 'Sorry, Miss,' wailed Frankie.

'It's no good being sorry, Frankie. Not while you're still doing it. Kindly stop your silliness this very second.'

'I'm doing my best, Miss.'

So he was. But by now he was as high as the drama-lights. 'Tell you what, Miss,' he said. 'I'll sort

of paddle about a bit. That might help.'

Perhaps it would have helped, too, if Frankie had been a better swimmer. As it was, waggling his arms and legs only made it worse. He swooped and zoomed about the hall like a giant wasp. Maybe that's why so many children went Ah! Ah! when he came too close.

'Fetch the caretaker,' shouted Mrs Jones above the noise. 'Ask him to pull Frankie down with one of his long window-poles.'

This sounded like a good idea. Yet it turned out to be a big mistake. To fetch the caretaker, you see, someone had to open the hall doors . . .

You're right.

The breeze from the open door sucked Frankie straight into the corridor. 'I can't help it, Miss,' he called over his shoulder.

'Stop him!' yelled Mrs Jones.

'Give us another head-over-heels, Frankie,' yelled the children.

'I don't want any trouble, Miss,' yelled Frankie. 'Honestly.'

Now this was quite true. Frankie hated being in trouble – which is why he felt so awful about the next two hours. Yes, that's how long it took the teachers and the helpers and the caretaker and Mrs Jones to catch him. Frankie flew in and out of

73

every classroom in the school.
Sometimes he bumped against
the ceiling, sometimes he
skimmed over the floor,
sometimes he dive-bombed the
desk-tops, sometimes he just
hovered over their heads in a
wasp-like way.

'He's just a great big bubble of
a boy,' said Mrs Jones. 'Be careful
how you grab him in case he
goes POP.'

The children loved it, of course.
Watching Frankie was better than
number work or word-books. It
was better than choosing-time
even. 'Why don't you loop some
string round his ankle, Miss?' one
of them said.

'Shush!' said the other kids.

They were too late. 'Good idea,'
said Mrs Jones. 'Why didn't I
think of that? And when I've
caught you, Frankie, I'll phone
your parents straight away. They
can keep you at home till you're
back to normal.'

Twenty minutes later, Frankie was on one end of a piece of string. His dad was on the other end and he wasn't very happy about it.

'What a show-up,' he said. 'It's bad enough having to fetch you from school, Frankie. Now I've got to tug you through the streets like a kid with a balloon. I feel such a fool.'

'So do I,' groaned Frankie. 'It's not my fault, Dad.'

'No? Some witch put a spell on you, I suppose?'

'Funny you should say that, Dad –'

'Frankie, don't you dare! Telling fibs doesn't help. The

sooner I get you to the doctor the better.'

'The flying doctor?' asked Frankie. 'Like in Australia?'

'Frankie!'

'Sorry, Dad.'

Frankie could see his dad wasn't in the mood for jokes. Neither was he, really. It wasn't much fun feeling like a fish caught on a fishing-line – except a fish doesn't get bumped against chimney-pots and snagged against the branches of trees.

'It's horrible,' said Frankie. 'All I can see is the *top* of everything – cars, people, traffic lights. I hate it.'

He didn't like being pointed at,

either. 'What have you got there?'
asked a policeman. 'A kind of
kite?'

'No,' said Dad. 'It's Frankie.'

'Is it a model aircraft?' asked a
boy at the bus-stop. 'Can I have a
go, mister?'

'No, it's not,' Dad said crossly.
'And no, you can't.'

'Me want one – me want one – me want one!' said a toddler in a buggy.

'Hard luck,' said Dad.

'Want it! Want it! Want it!' the toddler shrieked.

'See what you've done, Frankie?' Dad grumbled. 'This

daft trick of yours is upsetting everybody. Your mum will have a fit when I tell her. And what can we do about it, that's what I'd like to know. Fly you from a flagpole? Peg you down like a tent? Buy you some heavy boots so you clump about like a deep-sea diver?'

Frankie didn't fancy any of these one little bit. Something else was bothering him as well. 'Dad?' he called.

'What's wrong now, Frankie?'

'The string round my ankle, Dad. It's coming loose.'

'What?'

'Quick, Dad! I'm slipping away!'

But Dad wasn't quick enough. Down fell the string and up floated Frankie.

Higher and higher and higher.

Soon Frankie's dad looked no bigger than a pencil.

Then a paper-clip.

Then a pinprick.

Eventually, Frankie couldn't see his dad at all. He could see more and more of the rest of the world, though – even if it did get smaller and smaller as he floated further and further away. 'How far will I go?' wailed Frankie. 'Beyond the mountains? Beyond the moon? Beyond the stars?'

Already he was level with the clouds. There was a smoky

sourness all round him,
swallowing him up. Now there
was nothing at all he could see.
Suddenly . . .

CLATTER!
BONK!
THUMPETTYCLONK!

Spinning round and round and
round, Frankie and whatever he'd
bumped into came fluttering back
to earth. They landed upside
down in the ditch near Frankie's
school. 'Hello,' said Frankie.

'I don't believe it,' said the
witch. 'It's you again.'

'Just like last time,' said
Frankie. 'In fact, *exactly* like last

time. For instance, witch, you can't move a muscle again.'

'How do you know that?'

'Because I've got your wand,' said Frankie.

He rolled over and sat up. With one hand he held tight to a clump of grass to make sure he stayed on the ground. With his other hand he held up a stick – a stick like a long, bony finger. The witch licked her lips. 'Well done, Frankie,' she said. 'I always reckoned you were a smart lad.'

'I am now,' said Frankie.

'What do you mean by that, I wonder?'

'I mean I've learned my lesson,' said Frankie. 'My teacher's no

good at catching flyaway kids,
but she knows all about witches –
and witches' wands.'

'Er . . . let's not be hasty,
Frankie. Can't you take a joke?'

'Oh yes,' said Frankie. 'Can
you?'

'Me?'

'Because I'm only teasing you,

witch. You thought I was going to snap your wand in half and get rid of your magic, didn't you? But I won't, witch. Not if you promise to break the spell and get me out of trouble.'

'Certainly,' the witch said.

'You really promise?'

'Definitely,' said the witch.

'OK,' said Frankie.

And again he flipped the stick into the witch's upside-down lap.

Would you have done that?

Frankie did.

So serve him right when the witch gave a great whoop of cackly laughter. 'I tricked you, Frankie. A witch *never* keeps her promise. Didn't your teacher tell

you that? Now you're really in trouble!'

'No, I'm not,' said Frankie. 'You are.'

'I am?'

'Because that stick isn't your wand, witch. It's only an ordinary stick. I was testing you – just like my teacher said. Here's your real wand.'

Frankie held up another stick. This one looked even more like a long, bony finger. This one really was the witch's wand.

'What are you going to do?' asked the witch.

'This,' said Frankie.

SNAP!

He broke the wand in half.

Straight away, he felt safe on the ground again. And straight away the witch was the same as anybody else – with no magic at all. 'Goodbye,' said Frankie.

'Goodbye,' said the ex-witch grumpily.

Don't ask me what happened to her. But she still had her pointed hat, her black cloak and her broom made of twigs, remember, so maybe she ended up at a fancy dress party after all.